THE VICAR OF
NIBBLESWICKE

VIKING
Published by the Penguin Group
Viking Penguin, a division of Penguin Books USA Inc.,
375 Hudson Street, New York, New York 10014, U.S.A.
Penguin Books Ltd, 27 Wrights Lane, London W8 5TZ, England
Penguin Books Australia Ltd, Ringwood, Victoria, Australia
Penguin Books Canada Ltd, 10 Alcorn Avenue, Toronto, Ontario, Canada M4V 3B2
Penguin Books (N.Z.) Ltd, 182–190 Wairau Road, Auckland 10, New Zealand

Penguin Books Ltd, Registered Offices: Harmondsworth, Middlesex, England

First published in Great Britain by Random Century Group Ltd., 1991
First American edition published by Viking Penguin, a division of Penguin Books USA Inc., 1992

1   3   5   7   9   10   8   6   4   2

Library of Congress Cataloging-in-Publication Data
Dahl, Roald.
The vicar of Nibbleswicke / by Roald Dahl ;
illustrated by Quentin Blake.   p.   cm.
"First published in 1991 by Random Century Group, Ltd."—T.p. verso.
Summary: The vicar's speech impediment leads to holy
hysteria in an otherwise quiet country parish.
ISBN 0-670-84384-9 (hardcover)
[1. Clergy—Fiction.   2. Humorous stories.]
I. Blake, Quentin, ill.   II. Title.
PZ7.D1515Vi 1992 [Fic]—dc20   91-28223 CIP AC
Printed in U.S.A.

ROALD DAHL

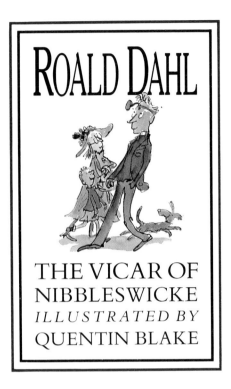

THE VICAR OF NIBBLESWICKE
ILLUSTRATED BY
QUENTIN BLAKE

VIKING

Once upon a time there lived in England a charming and God-fearing vicar called The Reverend Lee. When as a young man he first came to take up his duties in the small village of Nibbleswicke, there was for a while utter confusion and often genuine consternation among his devout parishioners.

What had happened was this. As a boy, Robert Lee had suffered from severe dyslexia. However, guided by the Dyslexia Institute in London and helped by some excellent teachers, Robert made such

splendid progress that by the time he was eighteen his writing and reading were both more or less normal and he was able to gratify his ambition to go into training for the ministry.

All went well and by the time he was twenty-seven Robert Lee had become the Reverend Lee and had been appointed to his first important job as vicar of Nibbleswicke.

During the drive down to Nibbleswicke in his old Morris

1000, it suddenly dawned upon him that for the first time in his life he was going to be all on his own. He began to get nervous. Would he be equal to running a parish? The previous vicar, as he knew, had died in harness and there would be nobody there to guide him.

When he eventually arrived at the vicarage, the only person there to greet him was a rather severe middle-aged daily woman who

showed him where things were in
the house and then left abruptly.

Oh dear, thought poor Robert
Lee as he lay in bed that night try-
ing to sleep. Will I really be able to
cope with this job? Weddings,
funerals, christenings, Sunday
Schools, the organist, the verger,
the church committee, the choir,
the bell-ringers and above all the
dreaded sermons . . . His mind

whirled. He began to sweat. And it is clear now that sometime during that horrible night something must have gone *click* in his brain and stirred up in some way vestiges of the old dyslexia that was lying there dormant, because the next morning when he got up he was suffering, although he did not know it himself at the time, from a very peculiar illness. It wasn't dyslexia but it was clearly related in some way to those old dyslexic problems. The way it affected him was as follows:

He would be talking to somebody and suddenly his mind would subconsciously pick out the most significant word in the sentence and reverse it. By that I mean he would automatically spell the word backwards and speak it in that way without even noticing what he had done. For example, trap became part, drab became bard, God became dog, spirit became tirips and so on. I repeat that he was not aware of what he was doing and therefore he never thought to correct himself.

When the Reverend Lee got up on that first morning, he found a note left by the verger on his desk politely suggesting that he make a start in his new parish by calling right away upon the wealthiest and most fervent supporter of the church in Nibbleswicke. This, the note added, was a maiden lady by the name of Miss Arabella Prewt.

Miss Prewt had recently footed the bill for one hundred new hassocks for the church, each one filled with sponge-rubber which was very easy on the knees, and the verger hinted that if the vicar played his cards right, the lady might be good for an even larger donation in the near future.

Very well, the Reverend Lee told himself. I'd better call on Miss Prewt right away, and he decided, so as to appear more friendly and informal, to leave off his dog-collar and to dress in mufti.

Setting off on foot, he soon found Miss Prewt's large Edwardian house, which was called "The Haven", and he rang the bell. The door was opened by

Miss Prewt herself, a tall thin female who stood bolt upright and whose mouth was like the blade of a knife.

"My dear Miss Twerp!" cried the Reverend Lee. "I am your new rotsap! My name is Eel, Robert Eel."

A small black-and-white dog appeared between Miss Prewt's legs and began to growl. The Reverend Lee bent down and smiled at the dog. "Good god," he said. "Good little god."

"Are you mad?" shouted Miss Prewt. "Who are you and what do you want?"

"I am Eel, Miss Twerp!" cried the vicar, extending his hand. "I am the new rotsap, the new raciv

of Nibbleswicke! Dog help me!"

Miss Prewt slammed the door in his face.

Things went from bad to worse. Soon the entire village was convinced that the new vicar was completely barmy. Pleasant and

harmless, they said, but completely and utterly barmy.

On one occasion the Reverend Lee walked into the village hall where the local ladies were holding their weekly knitting sessions, knitting sweaters for sailors in the Merchant Navy. "How lovely!" he cried. "How clever you all are! Each of you stink!"

Matters came to a head on the

following Saturday when the Reverend Lee met a small group of women who he was supposed to be preparing for their First Communion.

"The only thing I'm not sure about," said Mrs. Purgativa, "is whether you are supposed actually to drink the wine when the chalice is offered to you. If so, how much should one drink? What I mean is, should it be a good gulp or just a little sip?"

"Dear lady," cried the vicar, "you must never plug it! If everyone were to plug it the cup would be empty after about four goes and the rest of them wouldn't get any at all! What you must do is pis. Pis gently. All of you, all the way

along the rail must pis, pis, pis. Do you understand what I mean?"

They didn't, and the meeting broke up in disorder. Yet the Reverend Lee was too nice and gentle a man for anyone to bear any deep malice towards him. They couldn't believe he was being deliberately obscene. There was something wrong somewhere but none of them could say what it was.

Then came the first Sunday morning service, a great occasion for the village and a greater one for the vicar. The service turned out to be an amusing business because the vicar kept peppering his sentences with the most extraordinary words. They weren't obscene, nor did these words turn themselves into other words that meant anything at all; except in the case of one or two like 'dog' for 'God'. Very few words *do* make sense when spelled backwards, and the result of this was that the nervous young man got away with it. In fact, most of the congregation found the zany, word-crazy service

a rather welcome change from the old routine of well-worn phrases. It was rather fun, for instance, to hear him intoning, "and forgive us our sessapsert as we forgive those that ssapsert against us" rather than the other old thing. So on the whole the service went well and was voted very jolly indeed. Everyone was pleased with the new eccentric young vicar.

Then came the bombshell. When the service was over and "the blessing of Dog Almighty" had been given, the vicar stepped forward to the front of the altar rail and spoke as follows:

"Dear people, it is hardly my place as a newcomer to start making rules so early in my incumbency, but there is just one thing I feel I must mention. The road outside our little church is exceedingly narrow and as you know there is hardly room for two vehicles to pass each other. Therefore I feel it only right to ask members of the congregation not to krap all along the front of the church before the service. It is not only unsightly but it is also dangerous. If you all krap at the same time all along the side of the road you could be hit by a passing car at any time. There is plenty of room for you to do this alongside the church on the south side if you feel you must."

The silence that greeted this announcement was like the end of

the world and the poor vicar walked out of the church with not one kindly eye looking up to meet his.

In the end it was the local doctor who guessed what was wrong. "What you've got," he said, "is a very rare disease called Back-to-Front Dyslexia. It is very common among tortoises who even reverse their own name and call themselves esio trots. Fortunately," went on the good doctor, "there is a simple cure."

"Tell me!" cried the vicar. "Oh please tell me!"

"You must walk backwards while you are speaking; then these back-to-front words will come out frontwards or the right way round. It's common sense."

The cure worked miraculously. There were problems, of course. The main one was that the poor chap couldn't see where he was going without twisting his head over his shoulder, which was painful. But by attaching a small rear view mirror to his forehead with an elastic band, he overcame this difficulty. Sermons were also awkward, but the congregation very soon grew accustomed to seeing their vicar walking backwards round and round the pulpit while he was preaching. In fact, it added a nice, crazy touch to what was normally a dreary proceeding. In the end, the Reverend Robert Lee got so good at walking backwards that he never walked forwards at all, and for the rest of his life he became a lovable eccentric and a pillar of the parish.

When I first, at the invitation of Tom Maschler of Jonathan Cape, produced a set of sample drawings for Roald Dahl's book *The Enormous Crocodile* it had not occurred to me – I don't think it had occurred to any of us – that we were embarking on a collaboration that would extend over fifteen years and a dozen books. It's a collaboration of which I am proud and of which I have a lot of memories. Memories, of course, of discussion of pictures, of the subjects for pictures, of the interpretation of characters; most often carried out in the sympathetic atmosphere of Gipsy House, in the midst of the Dahl family. But other associated memories too, such as those Christmas readings which Roald used to give at the National Theatre. His audience filled one of the great auditoria – the Lyttelton or the Olivier; but nevertheless Roald – rooting in his old leather briefcase for the pages of an as yet unpublished story – seemed perfectly at ease; perfectly able to talk as though he were talking to each person individually. And after the performance, the signing of books. No children's author can surely have signed as many books as Roald Dahl: the queue of the National Theatre would be across the foyer and down the stairs; and though it might take two hours, everyone had a word and a signature. This concern for his readers and readiness to be available to them didn't end there. There were, for instance, replies to thousands of letters, both to children and teachers, with specially-written poems regularly renewed; and endless visits to schools and libraries.

And as well as generosity with time there were other kinds of generosity, works and gifts for charities and other institutions. They were private, not much talked about. But Roald had asked me to assist him in one or two projects for charity – a Christmas card for Great Ormond Street Hospital, for instance – and so it wasn't altogether a surprise to hear that familiar voice on the telephone, early last year, asking me if I'd be prepared to illustrate something that he was writing for the Dyslexia Institute. What *was* surprising was to hear what was being offered: the auction of all rights, worldwide, for the period of copyright. It's a privilege to be associated, among our many collaborations, with Roald in this book; a landmark of both his concern for people and his passionate belief in the importance of reading.